MaLik
Has A Gift

By Dionne L. Grayson

Malik Has A Gift: The Children's Gift Series
Copyright © 2021 Dionne L. Grayson
ISBN: 978-1-952327-47-6
Library of Congress Control Number: 2021902319

To request permissions, contact the author at info@buildingyourdreamsllc.com

Printed in the USA
T.A.L.K. Publishing, LLC
5215 North Ironwood
Suite 200 J
Glendale, WI 53217
publishwithtalk.com

DEDICATION

To all the fathers, mothers, and guardians
who are raising children with gifts - You have the
awesome responsibility of cultivating what has
been placed inside each of them. I pray for
your understanding and wisdom as you help
propel them into what they were designed to do.
My hope is that this book will spark something
as you move forward with your child(ren) in
exploration, exposure, and guidance.
Let's look inside and see!

This Book BeLongs To:

_____

1

Malik has a gift!
Let's look inside and see!

2

$$10 + 4 = 14$$
$$12 - 6 = 6$$
$$11 + 14 = 25$$

Malik has a gift!
And it's for you and me!

5

Malik has a gift!
It's what he loves to do!

6

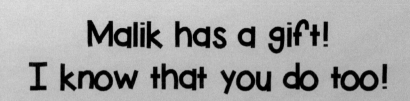

Malik has a gift!
I know that you do too!

Multiply, divide, add, and subtract...

10 + 4 = 14

12 - 6 = 6

11 + 14 = 25

11

Malik loves math and that's a fact!

Math is Malik's gift,
his gift for you and me!

14

$$10 + 4 = 14$$
$$12 - 6 = 6$$
$$11 + 14 = 25$$

Malik's gift is for the world,
for all of us to see!

A math teacher or accountant
are careers that he can choose.

19

They all have Malik's gift,
this really is good news!

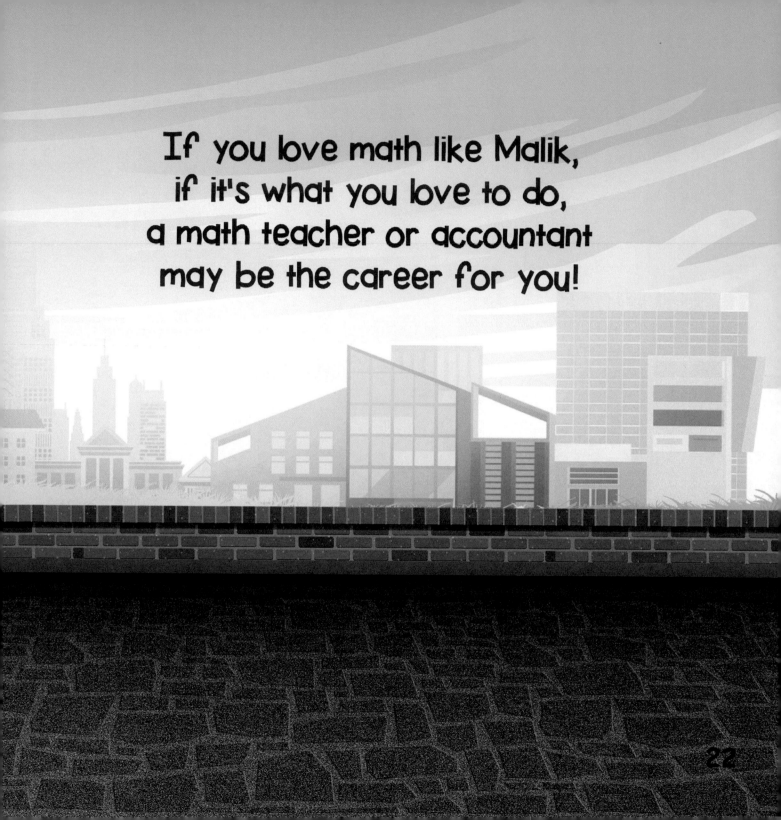

If you love math like Malik,
if it's what you love to do,
a math teacher or accountant
may be the career for you!

Math Teacher

$$10 + 4 = 14$$
$$12 - 6 = 6$$
$$11 + 14 = 25$$

A math teacher teaches mathematics to children.

Accountant

An accountant keeps track
of the money details for
a person or a company.

25

Will you please help Malik solve these problems?
Please point to the correct answer.

12 - 6 =
14 - 7 =
6 + 4 =
4 + 3 =
10 - 2 =
9 - 1 =

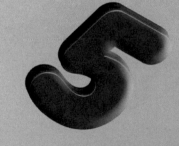

26

THE END

Made in the USA
Middletown, DE
29 October 2021

51270143R10020